Eddie's Kingdom

For Lucinda Hobart

1944—2002

www.houghtonmifflinbooks.com

The text of this book is set in triplex.
The illustrations are colored pencil and paint on paper.

Library of Congress Cataloging-in-Publication Data

Johnson, D. B. (Donald B.), 1944-
Eddie's kingdom / by D. B. Johnson.
p. cm.
Summary: After Eddie draws a picture of his apartment building neighbors, they all begin to get along with each other.
ISBN 0618-56299-0
[1. Neighbors—Fiction. 2. Interpersonal relations—Fiction. 3. Drawing—Fiction. 4. Apartment houses—Fiction.] I. Title.
PZ7.J6316215Ed 2005
[E]—dc22
2004013187

ISBN-13: 978-0618-56299-2

Manufactured in the United States of America
WOZ 10 9 8 7 6 5 4 3 2 1

Eddie's Kingdom

by D.B. Johnson

Houghton Mifflin Company Boston 2005

This is a picture of me,

King Eddie, on the second floor of my

kingdom. I drew it myself.

I only used to draw trees and cars and

buildings and animals.

Until yesterday I didn't try to draw

people. They were always fighting

with each other and yelling at me.

But yesterday I decided to draw a

picture of everybody in my building.

I took my pencil and a roll of
paper, and I rang the bell next
door at Apartment **4**.

"Are you the kid who bangs
the ball on my wall?"
Mrs. **4** growled.

I said I was Eddie, and I was
sorry about the ball, but I was
drawing a picture of everybody
in the building. Could I draw
her picture?

She unlocked her door
and let me in.

Mrs. **4**'s walls were covered with old paintings, all hanging crooked
(because of my ball banging, she said). I unrolled my paper, and I drew Mrs. **4**.

As I was going out the door, she said, "Don't draw that stinker upstairs next to me in your picture. He leaves his trash everywhere!"

I walked up to the third floor,
and I picked up all the trash outside
Apartment **5**. When I rang the bell,
Mr. **5** opened his door.

"Are you the kid who's always setting
off the smoke alarm?" he grumbled.

I said I was Eddie, and I was sorry about
the smoke alarm, but right now I was
drawing a picture of everybody
in the building. Could I draw his picture?

He let me in.

Mr. **5** was cooking noodles in a big pot and hanging them on the back of a chair.

As soon as I finished drawing his picture, he told me again to stop filling up the building with smoke.

Well, I wasn't making all the smoke. It was coming from his neighbor in Apartment **6**. I knocked at the door.

"Hey," said Mr. **6**, "are you the kid who plays that loud rock music? It drives me crazy!"

I said I was Eddie, and I was sorry about the music, but I was drawing a picture of everybody in the building. Could I draw his picture?

He let me in.

Mr. **6** was barbecuing chicken in his living room. I opened all the windows to let out the smoke so I could draw his picture. When I finished, I told him that if he'd cook out on the flat roof, I'd turn down the music.

He was mad the whole time we carried his barbecue grill up to the roof.

And then he yelled at me again. He looked as if he was going to chew my ear off.

It wasn't my music that was loud. It was coming from Apartment **1**, so I pounded on the door.

The music was so loud Mr. **1** had to shout. "ARE YOU THE KID IN APARTMENT **2** WHO MAKES HIS SISTER SCREAM? SHE'S SO LOUD, I CAN'T HEAR MY MUSIC!"

I said I was Eddie, and I was sorry about the screaming, but I was drawing a picture of everybody in the building. If he let me in, I'd draw him too.

I gave Mr. **1** earphones so he could listen to his music as
loud as he wanted while I drew his picture.

As I was leaving, he told me to stop hitting my sister.

It wasn't my sister screaming—
it was the baby in Apartment **2**.
So I took my best ball out of my
pocket, and I knocked on the door.

When Mrs. **2** saw my ball, she
growled, "Are you the kid in Apartment **3** who bangs that ball on my
ceiling? It wakes up my baby!"

I said I was Eddie, and I was sorry
about the ball, but I was drawing a
picture of everybody in the building.
Could I draw her picture?

She let me in.

I gave my ball to the baby to keep her happy while I drew Mrs. **2**. As soon as I was done, she told me that if I had to bounce my ball, I should only do it on the wall of that old grouch upstairs, Mrs. **4**.

I rolled up my paper and left. My picture was done!

The big flat roof was the best place to show everybody my picture. I hung it up and I covered it with the sheet from my bed. Then I made a sign for the front door.

BIG SHOW
ON THE ROOF
TONIGHT at 6
A PICTURE OF
EVERYBODY IN
THE PEACEABLE
BUILDING
BY Eddie

At six o'clock Mr. **1** and Mr. **5** clomped up to the roof. Mr. **6** sprang up the stairs behind them. Mrs. **4** came next, then Mrs. **2** with her screaming baby. They all left each other alone and looked around for something to eat. I didn't have anything to feed them. They were ready to bite each other's heads off, so I thought I'd better hurry up and show them my picture.

Everybody moved in close to see.
They were quiet. Even the baby stopped
screaming.

I pulled the sheet off.

Mr. **6** was the first to laugh. He roared out loud. "I didn't know I looked so scary," he said. "Look at my hair!"

"My nose is so long!" Mrs. **4** laughed.

"Hey, we've both got horns!" Mr. **5** said to Mr. **1**.

Then everybody laughed together and clapped each other on the back. I guess they never saw themselves being animals before!

MRS.4

Today you can hear laughing in my building. People are smiling at each other. And when they see me, they laugh and point. "Hey, Eddie," they say, "you're the KING!" They love my drawing because the animals look funny.

But I like my picture for a different reason. I like that, in my kingdom, the bear isn't chasing the goat, the lion isn't biting the ox, and the wolf isn't growling at me.